"Hello, Thumper!"
said Bambi.
"Hi-ya, Bambi!"
said Thumper.
"Whatcha wanna play?"

D0608114

"Well," said Bambi,
"how about . . ."
"Hide-and-Seek!"
cried Thumper.

"One, two, three,
four . . ." counted Bambi
while Thumper scampered
off to hide.

"Here I come!" called Bambi.
"Now, where could he be . . .?"
Aha! Was that a bunny behind the bush?

No. It was Momma Mouse
hiding her napping babies.
"Ssh!" she warned.

Was that Thumper up in a tree?

No. It was a squirrel
hiding nuts.

Was that Thumper making a noise
by the stream?

No. It was a frog snuggled up
in a water lily.
"Ribbit!"

Was that a bunny tail behind the log?

No. It was a woodpecker
looking for bugs. Tap, tap, tap!

Bambi lay down to rest.
Where could Thumper be?

Suddenly, a clump of flowers said, "Achoo!"

"That's called
Hide-and-Sneeze!"
giggled Bambi.

"Let's play again!"
laughed Thumper.